OTHER BOOKS BY CUBE KID

Diary of an 8-Bit Warrior
Diary of an 8-Bit Warrior: From Seeds to Swords
Diary of an 8-Bit Warrior: Crafting Alliances
Diary of an 8-Bit Warrior: Path of the Diamond
Diary of an 8-Bit Warrior: Quest Mode
Diary of an 8-Bit Warrior: Forging Destiny
Tales of an 8-Bit Kitten: Lost in the Nether
Tales of an 8-Bit Kitten: A Call to Arms
Diary of an 8-Bit Warrior Graphic Novel
Diary of an 8-Bit Warrior Graphic Novel: An Ominous Threat
Diary of an 8-Bit Warrior Graphic Novel: Another World
Diary of an 8-Bit Warrior Graphic Novel: Battle for the Dragon

• CUBE KID •

A NOOB'S DIARY OF AN 8-BIT WARRIOR

STORY ADAPTED BY
LAURA RIVIÈRE AND PIRATE SOURCIL

ILLUSTRATED BY
JEZ

COLORED BY
ODONE

Andrews McMeel
PUBLISHING®

Translated by Tanya Gold and based on the series Journal d'un Noob written
by Cube Kid © 2022, 404 éditions, an imprint of Édi8, Paris, France.

Story by Pirate Sourcil, novelization by Laura Rivière, illustrations
by Jez, color by Odone, and layout by Alex Mahé.

Minecraft is a Notch Development AB registered trademark. This book is a work of fiction
and not an official Minecraft product, nor approved by or associated with Mojang. The other
names, characters, places, and plots are either imagined by the author or used fictitiously.

Andrews McMeel Publishing, a division of Andrews McMeel Universal
1130 Walnut Street, Kansas City, Missouri 64106 www.andrewsmcmeel.com

23 24 25 26 27 SDB 10 9 8 7 6 5 4 3 2 1

ISBN: 978-1-5248-8240-2 (Paperback)
ISBN: 978-1-5248-8414-7 (Hardback)

Library of Congress Control Number: 2022947528

Made by:
RR Donnelley (Guangdong) Printing Solutions Company Ltd.
Address and location of manufacturer:
No. 2, Minzhu Road, Daning, Humen Town,
Dongguan City, Guangdong Province, China 523930
1st Printing — 3/06/2023

ATTENTION: SCHOOLS AND BUSINESSES
Andrews McMeel books are available at quantity discounts with bulk purchase
for educational, business, or sales promotional use. For information, please
e-mail the Andrews McMeel Publishing Special Sales Department:
sales@amuniversal.com.

I live in a village of **scaredy-cats!** We've built high walls to protect ourselves from monsters. They're everywhere at night. And we like to stay safe and scared in our homes instead of facing them! It's <u>RIDICULOUS</u>. I'd rather fight, face these monsters so they finally leave us alone. But nobody takes me seriously in the village.

1

One of the reasons why is my name. Why did my parents think calling me **Runt** was a good idea?! With that kind of name, of course everyone thinks I'm **a noob** . . . But if I could battle a monster, they'd finally see me as I really am: **a WARRIOR!**

But sadly, villagers never become warriors. All they care about is staying safe, cooped up in the village and earning emeralds! Everyone tells me that I should be a farmer like my parents, have a **"good job worthy of a villager."** But I dream of more.

STEVE is my idol. He's a warrior, and he's **SO COOL**. He's got style and a diamond sword he can defeat any monster with! That's so much cooler

than being a farmer, isn't it?

I'm still far away from that dream . . .

I CAN'T STAND THE THOUGHT OF BECOMING A FARMER. I WANT TO BE A WARRIOR, JUST LIKE STEVE!

BUT VILLAGERS NEVER BECOME WARRIORS.

This morning, I made a **HUGE mistake** at school. We were doing a really simple mining exercise. **BUT** I forgot to repair my pickaxe! Of course it broke and went flying toward the teacher's head!

Luckily, he wasn't hurt. But my pride wasn't as lucky. The whole class made fun of me. **Runt the <u>noob</u> strikes again!**

This afternoon, we had the only cool class of the week, **Mob Defense!**

"Today we're going to study **endermen**," the teacher said.

All the other students **shivered**. Not me. I was excited.

"They're dangerous creatures that will attack you if you look them in the eye," she continued. "Despite that, warriors hunt them down **for those very eyes**! That's because an **eye of ender** can open a portal to the End, **the dragon's lair**."

I took **meticulous** notes. (I learned this super fancy word in class yesterday. It means something like "careful.") To be honest, I **pay more attention** and I **focus more** in this class than anywhere else.

"What are villagers supposed to do if we run into an enderman?" the teacher asked.

Max, a kid in class who likes making fun of me, said we should sell him pants, because with legs that long, we'd make a lot of emeralds!

Of course, **everyone laughed.** Except me. This is a **serious topic!**

I couldn't help myself. "No! We attack them! **WE ATTACK THEM!**" I yelled.

The teacher covered her mouth in shock. "None of that! Attack an enderman?! **Never!** If you see one, **run**! Do you hear me, Runt?"

Everyone looked at me and **laughed**. None of them think I could be a warrior. And I'm going to prove them all wrong! I'm tired of it.

That was it. I decided to **get out of there** that night.

My friend Stump didn't think it was a good idea. "We're **NOT ALLOWED** to leave the village, Runt!" he said.

I told him it would be fine, that Steve had taught me how to craft a **wooden sword** when he was last here.

Stump thinks I'm such a noob. But I know how to defend myself! I even said he could come with me, but of course **that big chicken** said no. I guess **I can only count on myself!**

Later that evening, I packed my bag, making sure I didn't forget my wooden sword. I waited until it was dark out and my parents' backs were turned to sneak out of the house.

I was trying to make as little noise as possible when suddenly . . .

"RUNT!!"

I jumped out of my skin and turned around. **It was Stump!**

"**Not so loud!** Can't you tell I'm trying to sneak out?!"

"Exactly," he replied. "I wanted to **say goodbye!**"

"Thanks . . . **Wait!** What do you mean, **goodbye?!**"

9

"You're going out there at night with a wooden sword to fight all those monsters . . . Sorry, but I wouldn't bet an emerald on you making it back in one piece."

Thanks, Stump.

He walked with me to the village wall, then sold me a ladder to climb up it. (Villagers don't change their ways, even for friends.)

Once up there, I saw the moonlit horizon stretch before me.

Out there was adventure! I finally felt like I was somewhere I belonged.

That didn't last. Once I was outside the village, it got really dark. At first, everything was fine. Then

. . . "BLUUUURRRRP!" I heard **a TERRIBLE noise!**

I started shaking all over. I turned around and was face to face with **A ZOMBIE!**

A real one, all green, wearing torn clothes, **disgusting** and smelly. **Gross!** I closed my eyes for a few seconds.

What if Stump was right?

What if my wooden sword wasn't enough?

No, he was wrong!

I am a <u>**WARRIOR**</u>!

I tightened my grip on the handle of my sword and bravely ran forward . . . then turned around and ran away **LIGHTNING FAST**—I've never run that fast—leaving most of my stuff behind.

Luckily, **my diary was** safe in my pocket. At least I didn't lose everything.

After that, I went back home, coming in less than an hour after sneaking out, **like a NOOB**. My parents were still at the dinner table when I got home!

My mother was **worried** and asked me to explain, but I couldn't. I just ran into my room without saying a word. I climbed into bed and curled into a ball still in my **torn and filthy** clothes.

I'm so embarrassed! Everyone was right about me!

I'm just a noob, a loser, a failure. A villager like all the others, incapable of defending himself, unable to even take down a lone lost zombie . . .

Nothing like Steve.

Steve, now there's a true HERO. He would have crushed that zombie in a matter of seconds.

Everyone's going to laugh tomorrow at school when Stump tells them how he tricked me into buying a ladder and how he saw me coming home only an hour later, **like a big loser**. Max is going to love this too!

I'll never be a **powerful warrior** like Steve. I might as well get used to the idea . . .

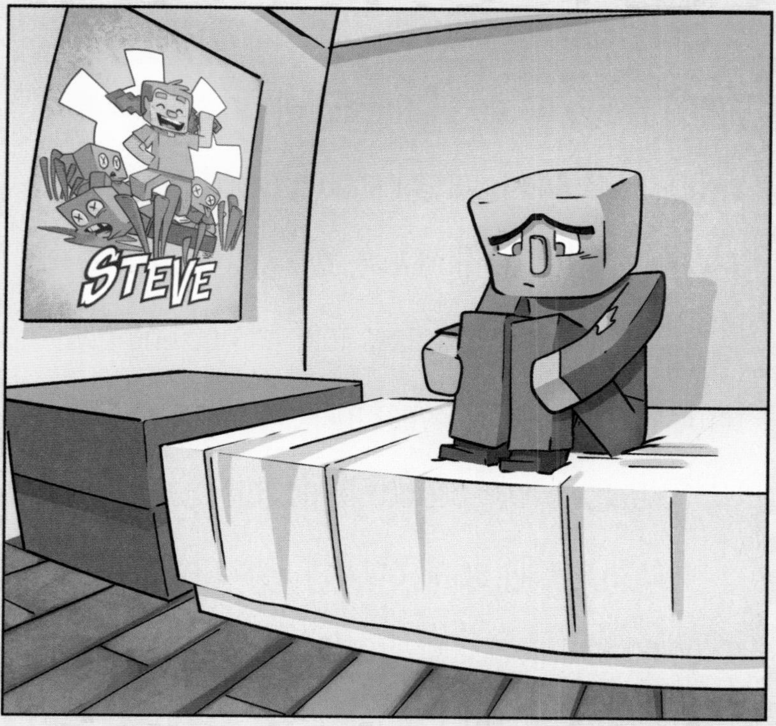
STEVE

TUESDAY

This morning, when I got up, I was **a bit less upset** than yesterday. My first big adventure **didn't really go as planned**. But I'm still in one piece, right? And I guess I should expect that being a warrior is **hard**. Otherwise, everyone would do it.

I bet Steve has bad days too. And **getting back up to fight again** is what makes a great warrior!

So that's what I decided to do this morning.

I wasn't really being brave. I was actually scared of going back to school. I didn't want to deal with Max or Stump making fun of me.

The next time they'd see me, I'd be a mighty warrior. Then they wouldn't laugh at me anymore.

They'd **BOW** before me! But before that, I'd have to prove myself.

I made myself another bag to replace the one I lost yesterday, put everything I needed in it, and crafted **a new wooden sword.**

It's not the most effective weapon, but it works.

When I was ready, I walked out of my room, trying to look **NORMAL.**

"Have a good day, Runt. See you tonight!" my parents said.

"Yeah, see you TONIGHT!"

They looked at me funny, so I rushed off, slamming the door behind me. So much for not drawing attention to myself.

Instead of going to school, I headed out of **the village**. I hugged the village walls, trying to avoid everyone from school. I didn't want to bump into Stump, or worse, **Max.**

Luckily, I didn't encounter anyone, and I managed to slip quietly out of the village.

Once outside, I took a deep breath. **The monsters needed to watch out for me**

this time! I was more determined than ever. They were going to get it!

But first, before I attacked anyone, I had to find a quiet (and safe!) place to set up camp.

I soon found **the perfect place**, right at the edge of the forest, not too far from a series of caves.

I got to work. I carved out a small space in the rock. I even put in **a door!** Outside, I crafted a small furnace and made stools out of tree trunks. I made a few even though I was alone. You never know who you might bump into, and my mom says to **ALWAYS** be ready for someone to drop in.

Once I was done, I took a look at my camp. **It looked AWESOME.** I was almost sad that Stump wasn't there to see it. But I got over it quickly. I can't see Stump again until I've become a warrior, **a true one!** I was fine all alone anyway. I don't need anyone! Isn't Steve **on his own**? He can fend for himself, and I can too!

And it was about time to start that adventure! I wasn't going to fight any monsters just sitting by the fire.

I decided to check out one of the caves close to my camp first. It was **SO DARK** in there I could barely see a thing.

It took me a while to adjust to the darkness. (I even bumped into the walls a few times. **How embarrassing!**)

I walked for a long, **long, long time** . . .
and I still hadn't seen anyone! Not a soul in this
cave, not even a monster.

I let out a loud sigh.

I was about to give up when I came face to face
with a **WHOLE HORDE OF ZOMBIES.** Not one, not
two, not three, but **four stinking ZOMBIES.**

I learn from my mistakes. I thought about my
last encounter with a zombie and decided to do
what I did then, the only thing you can do when
face-to-face with zombies: **RUN!** (My teacher was
kind of right!)

I turned and fled from that cave so I could get
out of this **ALIVE!**

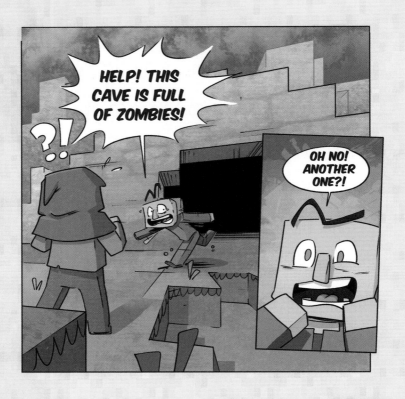

Exiting the cave, I yelled, "HELP!! THIS CAVE IS FULL OF ZOMBIES!!"

And who did I bump into outside? ANOTHER ZOMBIE! Or so I thought. I soon realized I was wrong.

It was just a strange guy with a big hood.

Phew! I apologized for thinking he was a zombie.

It must have been all that bright light right

after being in the cave. I couldn't see clearly.

He let out an awkward **laugh. "Ha ha!** No, I'm

just **Blurp**, a simple traveler!"

"I'm **Runt**. How smart to wear a hood like that!"

"Yeah, I realized monsters don't notice me as much like this!"

I wasn't surprised! If I thought he was a zombie, I bet monsters (who aren't always the brightest) also make that mistake. Real smart! I think I'm going to get along with this guy.

He does look **a bit odd** with his hood, and he looks a bit green. I wondered if he might be sick. Poor guy, he must have traveled far and probably didn't eat enough. So I invited him to come and have a bite with me at my new camp. He hesitated, then finally agreed.

"Nice camp you've got here!" he said when he arrived.

"Make yourself comfortable!"

We sat down, and I offered to cook him a chicken leg. He said he'd rather eat it **raw**.

That was really weird, but I'm trying to not judge. Maybe that's how they eat chicken in his village.

"You have a funny accent," I said. "Where are you from?"

"Umm . . . **the other side of the world!** I've come a long way."

He must be **really shy** because he seems to be searching for the right words and hesitating a lot before speaking. But he also seems really nice. So I'm not too worried.

"That's **so cool!** I just left my village," I told him. "I want to be the first villager to become **a warrior!**"

"**Impressive!** Is that why you were on the lookout for monsters?"

"Yep."

I didn't want to say more than that. I didn't want him to know that I ran away like a **GIANT COWARD** without defeating a single one of the monsters in the cave. I didn't want him to realize I was a joke. So I decided to tell him about my great quest instead.

"I was looking for **an enderman**."

ARE YOU OUT OF YOUR MIND? THEY'RE SUPER DANGEROUS!

"Are you **out of your mind?** They're super dangerous. Even us zom . . . the people where I'm from don't go near them!"

"**I don't have any choice!** I need one to get to **the End!** That's what a real warrior would do, right?"

Blurp nodded, looking **impressed**.

It made me so happy. That was the first time someone took me seriously when I talked about becoming a warrior. It was such a nice change from the people of my village. I'm glad I left!

Despite how **strange** he is, Blurp seems like a nice guy. I think the two of us are going to get along well. He might even become my friend, who knows? And just because Steve isn't part of a team doesn't mean I can't be. He's my idol, but I don't have to copy everything he does.

After dinner, I went to bed. This day had been **so tiring.** I deserved some rest. Blurp wanted to stay up a bit longer, so I wished him goodnight and fell asleep just like that.

One thing's for sure. Being a warrior is

EXHAUSTING!

This morning, when I got up, Blurp was already outside.

"You didn't sleep?" I asked.

"**Nope**, never at night," he replied.

This guy is <u>**SO WEIRD**</u>. He eats his food raw, and he doesn't sleep. **What planet is he from?**

I didn't say anything—I'm not about to mess with this new friendship—but I'll have to look into it. Because something's **NOT RIGHT**.

So I changed the subject, and we sat down to breakfast. We were quietly discussing our plans for the day when we heard a **SNAP** coming from the forest.

I turned my head, and suddenly, **THWACK! A HUGE ARROW** landed right at my feet. I yelled so loud!

Blurp and I jumped up to figure out where the attack was coming from.

It was a skeleton! It was ugly and gray, had a bow and arrow, and was getting ready to shoot at us again!

I tried to hand my wooden sword to Blurp so he could defend us, but he didn't seem to know what to do either.

"Go for it. **You're the warrior** here!" he said.

All the while, arrows were whizzing past our ears. I got knocked over in the confusion and when I looked up **THE HORRIBLE SKELETON WAS THERE,** right above me, about to **EAT ME.** I was so **scared** I couldn't even scream.

Luckily, Blurp found the courage to rush toward the skeleton, even though **HE DIDN'T EVEN HAVE A WEAPON.**

While the skeleton's back was turned, I grabbed my wooden sword from the ground and **STABBED him!**

My heart stopped for a few seconds, then we heard a **POOF!**

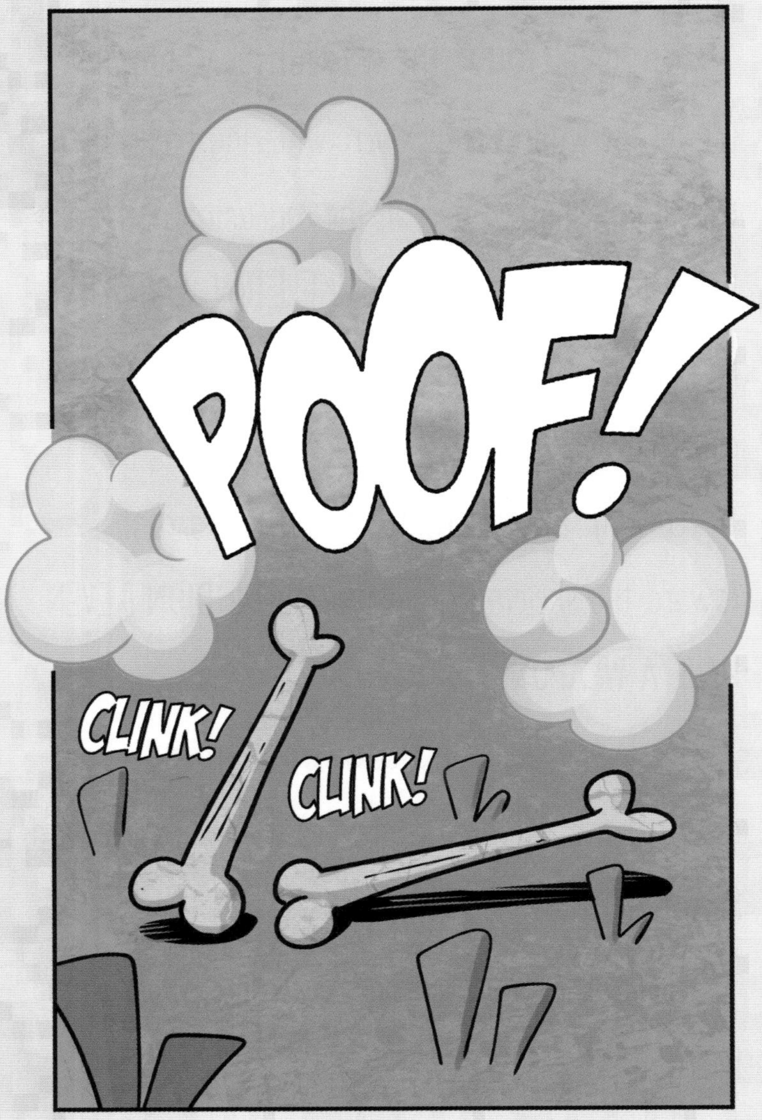
POOF!
CLINK!
CLINK!

Then the skeleton disappeared, almost completely evaporated, leaving only a couple of **his bones falling to the ground.**

"You okay, Runt?" Blurp asked me, a **worried** look on his face.

"**Nothing's broken.** Anyway, thanks, Blurp. Well done! You don't look like it, but you're **a true warrior!**"

I could swear I saw him blush from under his hood.

"You really think so?"

I didn't have time to answer him before **SNAP! SNAP!** More noises came from the forest.

"**AAAH!** What's that noise?" Blurp asked, hiding behind me.

"Of course. You're definitely a real warrior! **Heh heh!**"

I started worrying as the noise got closer. So I brandished my sword—check out my warrior vocabulary!—and prepared to face the danger.

That's when a **DANGEROUS WOLF** came out of the forest and pounced on one of the skeleton bones. I was about to attack it, but . . .

I stopped to think for a second—yes, I do that sometimes! The wolf was hiding in a bush, and I stepped forward, picking up **one of the bones** on the way.

"**Be careful!**" yelled Blurp. "He could be **dangerous!**"

But I wasn't listening to him anymore. I walked over to the wolf, holding out the bone. "Here! **This is for you!**"

And it **WORKED!** The wolf let himself be **coaxed out** right away. I was even able to pet his head, just like a nice little dog.

It was a good thing I paid attention in class! That's where I'd learned you can tame wolves with bones.

I never thought I'd have the chance to do it! If only Max could have seen that! The face he'd make! **Who's the NOOB** now?!

THAT'S RIGHT. NICE WOLF.

TAP! TAP!

Blurp didn't seem very comfortable around our new four-legged friend. I think he's **really cute**! But Blurp was being weird again.

I tried to make him feel better. "When they're tamed, they **protect us** from monsters! This is so cool!"

Blurp didn't seem to think it was all that great. He made a strange face.

Well, I'm not going to judge him, especially since he said something to me afterward that made me **VERY** happy.

"Looks like you've made a new friend," he said. "But even with the three of us working together, it won't be easy to defeat **an enderman**."

"Us?" I repeated. "Are you serious? You want to join me?"

"Of course! I'd love to join you on this adventure!"

"You saved me earlier. Maybe I'll be able to return the favor!"

THWAP! We shook on it and officially marked the beginning of our friendship.

I noticed Blurp's **greenish hand** and torn shirt again. I wondered what happened to him during his travels for him to end up like this. He must have come across a few monsters and eaten things that he shouldn't have!

The poor guy . . . It's a good thing he found me!

Together, **we'll be stronger** and better able to fight monsters. And I won't let him eat what he shouldn't!

At the end of that eventful day, we settled down around my little furnace for a **well-earned meal**. That many adventures in a day can make you hungry! We had chicken again so the wolf could have our leftovers.

During the meal, Blurp looked **a little distracted**. He must have been really deep in thought. He looked at everything strangely—me, the wolf, the chicken.

I was **so pooped** that I didn't have it in me to ask him about it. After dinner, I just went to bed.

I said good night to everyone and fell asleep **THEN AND THERE.** Rest is so important for warriors. I'm not messing around with that, especially since we're going to go looking for an enderman tomorrow. We have to be in **fighting shape** if we don't want things to go wrong. **I can't wait!**

My dream might soon come true . . .

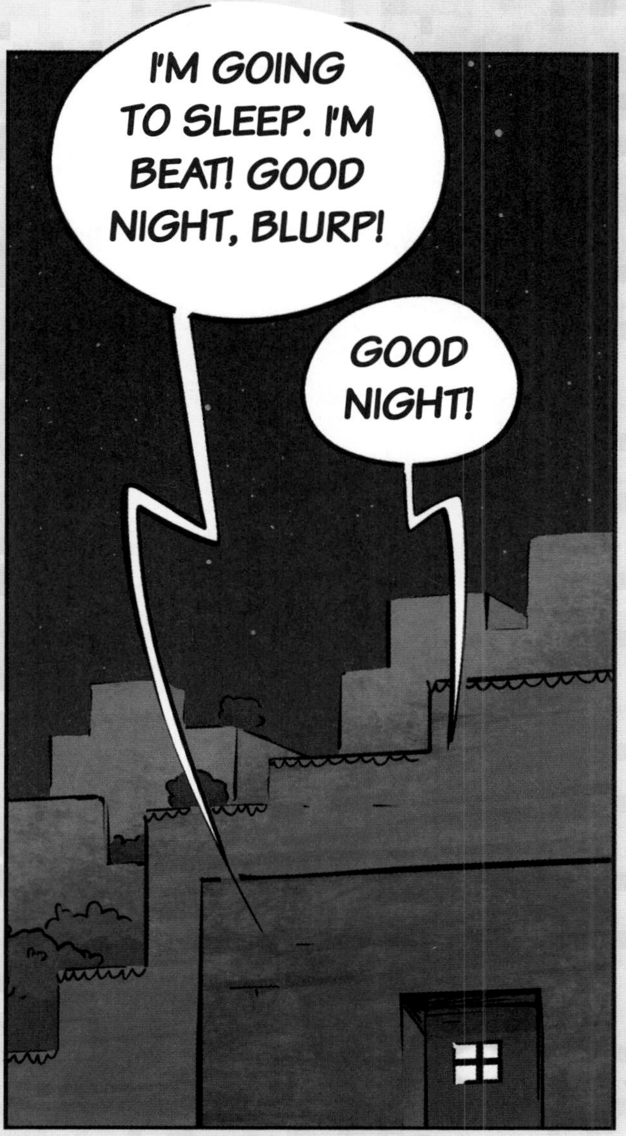
I'M GOING TO SLEEP. I'M BEAT! GOOD NIGHT, BLURP!
GOOD NIGHT!

This morning, I woke up **ready to go**. I felt so **much better** knowing that Blurp would help me go to the End! I was so excited, I got up at sunrise.

Blurp was already waiting for me outside.

"Look over there," I began. "I think it's an abandoned mine! In class, we learned that endermen like dark places. I think we should start there if we want to find one."

"**Let's go!**" Blurp said.

"Wolf, are you coming with us?"

"Woof!"

So we all headed for the mine! And it was **so dark in there!** Three steps in and I could barely see a thing. Well, I could see enough to notice the **GIANT SPIDER WEBS** hanging everywhere.

At one point, I walked right into one. <u>**SO GROSS!!**</u> Luckily, the spider wasn't there. I couldn't even imagine how big the one that made that web would be. Beside me, Blurp didn't look too happy.

"Are you sure this is **a good idea?**"

"**No.** But it's our best bet for finding an enderman."

He still didn't look convinced, so I tried a joke to lighten the mood. "What are you afraid of? Poo Screamers?"

He did not look amused. "You just made that monster up!"

And we continued through the mine.

The three of us kept going, **even though it was really dark**.

We followed the rail tracks, passing a few carts full of coal, until we came to what must have been the heart of the mine.

It was so much brighter there! **It was wild!** There was lava everywhere, flowing down the rock walls. It was **so cool!** And **so <u>dangerous!</u>**

In the center, there was this giant pool of lava (and not the kind of pool you want to swim in). To get to the other side, you had to go across this narrow stone bridge, barely wide enough for the three of us to walk across single file.

"Be careful! This bridge isn't stable," I warned Blurp.

"You're right," he replied. "**Let's turn around!**"

"That's not what I meant, Blurp!"

Turn around? When we were so close to our goal? No way! **I HAD TO find an enderman** no matter what. I wasn't going to give up so easily.

"Listen," I said. "Did you hear that?"

"What? No . . . I don't hear anything," answered Blurp.

"**Exactly!** I can't hear anything! No zombie noises! We'll be fine! **Come on!**"

I tried making Blurp feel safer, explaining that I was **VERY GOOD** at spotting zombies and that if there were any around, I would have spotted them

RIGHT AWAY. I don't know why, but he didn't seem to believe me. This guy seems to doubt everything . . .

So there I was, calmly walking across that narrow bridge, feeling pretty confident because of the lack of zombies, so I starting walking a bit more quickly and . . .

WhooOOOooossssh!

What was bound to happen happened. I fell crossing that **stupid bridge!** It felt like I was hovering in mid-air for a few seconds, my eyes fixed on the lava below . . .

"RUNT?!" Blurp screamed.

Somehow, I'd managed to grab the edge of the bridge with one hand on my way down.

"BLURP! **HELP!** I'M TOO YOUNG TO DIIIIIIIIIE!"

"HOLD ON!" he yelled.

The lava below was so hot, I felt the heat on my feet.

Blurp grabbed my hand and tried to pull me up. But he couldn't do it. I wasn't moving an **inch!**

I felt like the lava was getting closer. I **begged** Blurp to help me, but he wasn't strong enough. So I closed my eyes and got ready for the lava to take me . . . **when I felt a hand grab me and pull me up.**

"You okay, kid?"

I didn't even look up. I was too busy trying to catch my breath. I almost didn't make it!

"Is my bridge so ugly that you'd rather jump into the lava than walk across it?!"

I looked up at the person talking to me.

NO WAY!

<u>STEVE.</u>

It was Steve! My hero! My idol! And he was standing right there in front of me, a box under his arm and a sword tucked in his belt. STEVE, WHO'D SAVED ME FROM MOLTEN LAVA!

I couldn't believe it. It had been so long since I'd seen him. I was so happy!

So happy that I could barely put two words together.

"You two shouldn't be hanging out here. It's too dangerous for kids."

Okay, so that's not really what I wanted to hear from him.

"We're not kids, Steve! We're warriors," I finally managed to reply.

"If you say so! But you might want to follow my advice. I won't always be there for you!"

And then he just left, leaving us behind on his stupid bridge. I was a bit annoyed. I mean, **if I'd died**, it would have been because of his crappy bridge!

"You all right, Runt? Are you sure you want to keep going?" Blurp asked.

I shrugged and sighed. "Steve must have already **taken out all the monsters** around here! Still, this is too much adventure for one day. Let's get out of here . . . each in one piece!"

Blurp looked **relieved**. We walked back out of the mine, each of us carefully watching our step.

When we got outside . . .

GRRRRRRRR!

"Did you hear that?" Blurp asked.

"What?"

GRRRRRRRRR!

"Oh, that? It's just my stomach. I'm starving,
aren't you, Blurp?"

"Why yes . . ."

"When I'm hungry, I start to see food
everywhere! Like just looking at this bush . . . I'm
thinking of **a big pork roast! Mmmm!** Does
that ever happen to you?"

"Yes, yes it does," Blurp said.

He was **looking at me real funny** when he said that. For a second there, I thought he wanted to eat me! <u>**SCARY!**</u> The guy must have been starving.

I picked up the pace so we could find a place to set up camp and have a bite to eat. The wolf looked hungry, too, and I really didn't want **my friends to eat me!** Ha ha!

After a few minutes, we found **the perfect place**, a small cave carved into the rock.

"This place is great! Let's set up camp here," I said. "I'm going to craft us a furnace, then we can have some food."

While I was crafting a few things to make our new camp comfortable, Blurp went to get some firewood. The wolf wandered off into the forest too.

When Blurp came back, he had his arms full of logs. And the wolf came back **carrying a chicken**. We had everything we needed for dinner!

"Now we'll be safe! Monsters won't eat us tonight!" I told Blurp.

He looked like he was trying hard to focus and didn't answer me.

Sometimes I feel like he's avoiding talking about zombies and other monsters. **He must have gone through some bad stuff** during his travels to be that scared! Once we get to know each other a bit better, I think I'll try to talk to him about it.

After all, we're friends now, right? And friends talk about that kind of stuff.

At least **I think so** . . .

But for now, I'm going to get some sleep. It's getting late. And I bet we're going to have even more adventures tomorrow!

I can't wait!

This morning, I woke up **FEELING GREAT** and ready to take down any monsters that crossed my path!

We started off the day right with a big breakfast to fuel our adventure. We needed our strength!

We were sitting around the fire Blurp had made, the wolf eating at my feet, when I had an idea.

"I th'k we sh'd come up wif a nmm for 'm."

"I didn't get a word of that!" Blurp said.

I swallowed the rest of my breakfast and tried again. "We should come up with **a name** for him."

"That's right, he's on our team now," Blurp said.

"What do you think of . . . **Mobslayer?**"

Blurp made one of those **WEIRD** faces again, but the wolf seemed really happy.

"I think he likes it!" Blurp finally said, seeming to come to his senses.

After breakfast, we set off, determined to find an enderman.

Since leaving my village, I've seen so many **INCREDIBLE** things! Like the mines. They don't look like much from the outside, but once you get in them, it's **a whole new world!** The bright red lava casts shapes on the walls in the dark. It's scary, but it's beautiful too. And the outdoors are so cool. This whole area is **FULL** of cliffs and hills. And then there are all these forests. They're like giant playgrounds!

Before leaving my village, I had no idea that the outside world could be like this. My parents and teachers always talked about the monsters and how dangerous it all is, but never about how beautiful it is! **It's so sad** that they don't get to experience all this just because they're scared.

When I finally go back home, I'll have to tell them about everything they're missing! That'll show Max and Stump!

But we've still got a long way to go before then.

We hadn't seen a single monster that day. So Blurp and I took the opportunity to get to know each other a bit better. It felt like I've known him for a long time, but I didn't really know much about him. Since we'd been hanging out, we'd been so busy we hadn't really had the chance to talk much.

I decided to ask him about something that had been bugging me for some time. "So, Blurp, does everyone in your village . . . **look as sick as you?**"

"What do you mean, **sick?**"

"I don't know . . . I mean, you look **a bit green**. And you don't seem to like sunlight either. You hide under that hood. If someone did that in my village, we'd think they were unwell."

"**I'm not sick!** And neither are the people from my cave . . . from my village. Some of them look a bit . . . **scary**. But deep down, we're good people. You just have to dig a little."

"I hear you! It's the same at home for me. My crafting teacher is **TERRIFYING!**"

We sat down for a well-deserved break, and I took a picture of my parents out of my bag to show Blurp. He looked at it and made a **really weird** face again.

"Um . . . Is that your mom?"

"No, that's my dad! Do you have slime goo in your eyes or something?!"

I held out the picture again to point out my mom, but he still looked confused. He might not be sick, but he sure needs **glasses!**

MY MOM'S NEXT TO HIM.

OH YEAH . . .

Later that afternoon, as we continued our hunt

for an enderman, Blurp asked me about myself.

"Say, Runt, why did you **run away** from home?"

"**Well** . . . I always wanted to be a warrior,

and my parents weren't okay with that. So I left **to**

prove them wrong."

"I know what it's like when your family **doesn't**

accept who you are." Blurp sighed.

"**Oh yeah?** Do yours want you to stay a regular

villager too?"

"Um, yeah, **something like that.** My family's

worried, but it's mostly kids from school and the

others who live there who don't accept me . . ."

Then we were both quiet for a bit. It was a little bit awkward.

Then Blurp said, "Anyway, I'm glad I met you. It's hard being alone out here away from my cave . . . um, village!"

"Yeah, it's more fun as a team! You're a true friend, Blurp."

YOU'RE A TRUE FRIEND, BLURP.

Then there was a longer silence. That one was a

bit more **awkward.**

"**Well,**" I said, breaking the silence. "It's going

to be dark soon. We should find a place to set up

camp. My legs are like jelly!"

"We did walk a lot, didn't we? Let's settle down

here for the night. I'm sure we'll find an enderman

tomorrow."

Blurp, Mobslayer, and I found the perfect place

to spend the night, a small cave at the edge of the

forest. We had chicken for dinner again, then we

went to bed.

I don't think I've ever walked so much in my life! The

village is a long way behind me now, that's for sure.

Sometimes I wonder what my parents must be thinking—and Stump too. Did they go looking for me? Are they sad? Are they worried? Anyway, when I go back, they'll see that I'm **a <u>WARRIOR</u>**, a true one, and then they'll have to be proud of me.

I hope things work out for Blurp too. From what he told me, they don't seem to get him in his village either. At least now that we've met, we don't need them anymore. We've got each other. And, in the end, everyone will see how great we are. So **<u>there!</u>**

I was woken up by **a faint pink glow** outside the cave in the middle of the night. Blurp, as usual, was already (or still?) outside.

"**What in the world is that?**" I whispered. "Have you ever seen anything like it?"

"Are they fireflies?" asked Blurp.

"No, not even close."

They didn't look like fireflies at all. They were more like pink, **glowing** squares. They were so bright it was almost like being in daylight.

"Blurp, **look**! There's more!"

The pink lights moved quietly through the air, floating gently. They seemed to be coming from

71

something . . . or from someone.

"They don't look like they're **alive**. It's like they're just floating with the wind!" I said.

The lights led us into the forest.

"Think we should follow them?" I asked Blurp.

"I don't know. It could be **dangerous!**"

"Or maybe they'll lead us to treasure! Come on, Blurp!"

My friend seemed nervous and uncertain (as always), but since Mobslayer and I had already entered the forest, he had to come with us.

So the three of us went into the forest. It was **REALLY DARK** there, even with the floating lights. Somehow, I felt really sure of myself. I didn't feel afraid. Unlike Blurp, who kept **questioning** what we were doing.

He kept saying "I don't know about this," and "Don't you think we should turn around?" It was like that **FOREVER**, and it took everything I had to not yell at him.

I really like Blurp, but he can be a bit of **a scaredy-cat sometimes**.

So I tried to make him feel better the only way I could think of. "No, we're close. There are more of them!"

The deeper into the forest we went, the more lights there were. It was like they all planned to meet there! After walking for **HOURS**, I knew we'd finally made it.

"That's what I'm afraid of," Blurp muttered.

That's when **I SAW IT**. There, in the middle of a clearing, lit up by all those pink lights. **AN ENDERMAN!** A REAL ONE!

"SHHHHHH!" I said.

Blurp and I hid behind some trees, and Mobslayer followed our lead.

Slime goo! I never thought we'd find an enderman that quickly! He was even bigger and more terrifying than I could have imagined! I needed a moment to think . . .

I slowly peered around the tree to watch it for a few seconds. **And my eyes met the monster's . . .**

"EEEEEE**EEERRRREEEEE**!!" he roared.

"Oh no! I looked him in the eye! **We're dead!**"

I recovered quickly. I'm a warrior after all, right?

I decided to act like a warrior. I believed in myself

and took out my trusty wooden sword, ready to face

my enemy, to **LOOK HIM IN THE EYE.** But when I turned around, the clearing was empty. **He'd already teleported!** That's when I freaked out.

"**RUN!!!**" I yelled to my friends.

Blurp, Mobslayer, and I ran out of there **SO FAST.** We managed to get away from the enderman and make it out of the forest, but we were blinded by the light when we got there. It was already

morning! Luckily, my eyes adjusted in time to not

fall off **THE HUGE CLIFF** we were at the edge of!

"RUNT! **BEHIND YOU!!**" I heard Blurp shout

from behind me at the same time as a loud **ZAP!**

I turned around to see the enderman right there,

right in front of my face, and he tried to hit me.

HuuUUUUURR!!

By some miracle I dodged his attack and

didn't fall off the cliff.

Mobslayer and I were cornered. The monster was

in front of us, the cliff's edge behind. But we didn't

give up. We stood up to him. In the chaos of battle,

I dropped my sword. So I used my fists instead.

The wolf bared his fangs and growled. But the enderman didn't seem to care.

"EEEEEEEEERRRRREEEEE!!"

"**Beat it!**" Blurp shouted, coming up behind him.

The monster looked **surprised** and turned around suddenly, his arm slamming into me and sending me flying all the way to the edge of the forest. I hit the ground hard. I couldn't move or think.

In the distance, the battle was raging on. I could hear Blurp's voice calling out to me and the monster's roars.

"EEEEEEEEERRRRREEEEE!!"

I couldn't really understand what was happening. I could make out some of Blurp's words.

"Leave us alone! . . . a monster . . . like you . . . "

Then I heard Mobslayer growl, the monster struggle, and then Blurp yelling "NOOOOO**OOOOO**OOOOOO!"

It was at that point that my head cleared. I got up and walked over to Blurp, my head still aching, and asked him what happened.

"The enderman fell off the edge . . . and **he took Mobslayer with him**," Blurp said between sobs.

"NO! This . . . **this is horrible!!"** I yelled as I headed for the cliff's edge. "We have to save him!"

Then I turned back to Blurp. His hood had fallen off. I could see his face clearly for the first time.

A ZOMBIE!

Blurp is a ZOMBIE! HE HAS BEEN ALL ALONG!!

He had me fooled with his stories of a distant village and long travels!

I spotted my sword on the ground, grabbed it, and **STORMED** toward Blurp.

"**No! Wait!**" he said. "Please, Runt! Because of you I finally got to live my dream and leave my zombie days behind—to be like you!"

"You want to be **a villager**?" I asked, surprised.

"**Yes!** I don't want to be treated like a monster anymore. And even though I'm a zombie, we had fun, right?"

He wasn't wrong. But I was still SO **ANGRY** that he'd lied.

"You know that villagers don't like zombies . . ."

I took a **deep** breath.

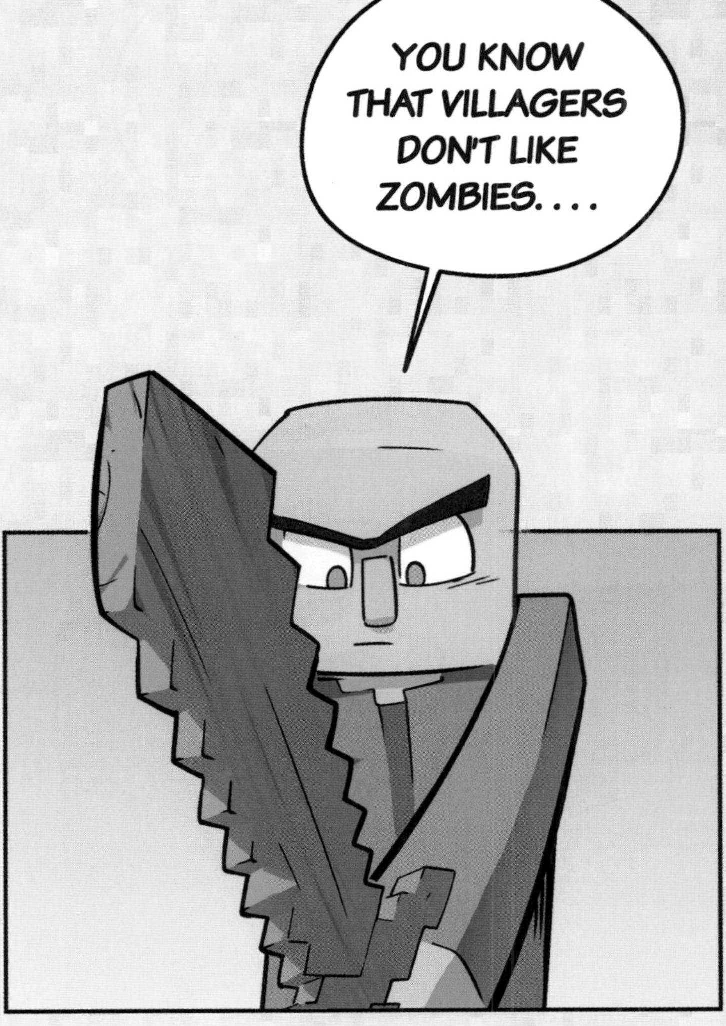
YOU KNOW THAT VILLAGERS DON'T LIKE ZOMBIES. . . .

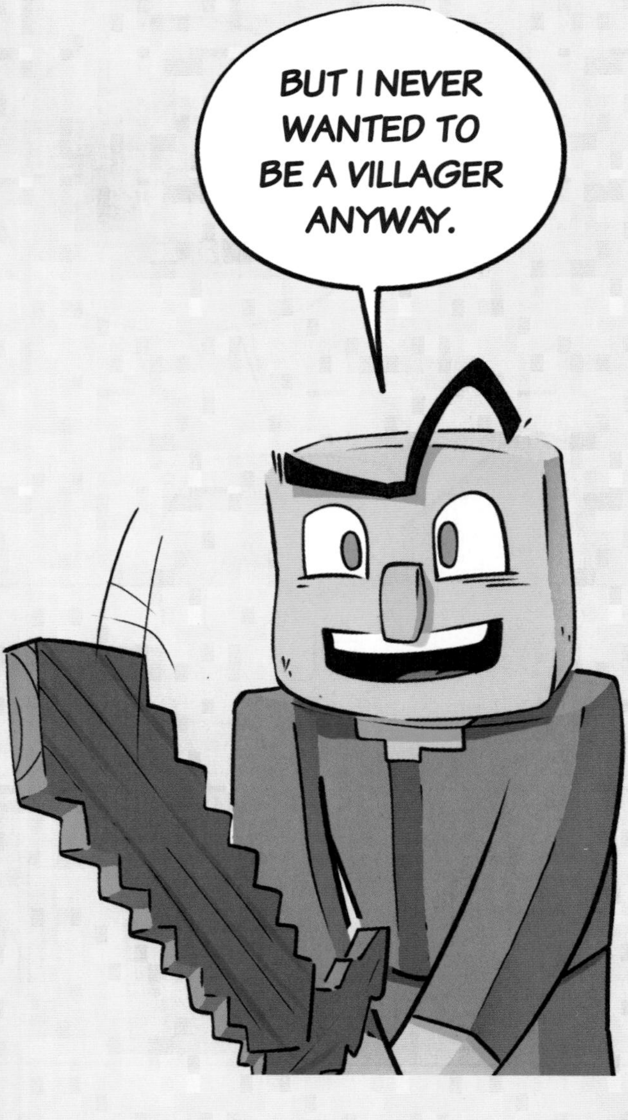
BUT I NEVER WANTED TO BE A VILLAGER ANYWAY.

". . . but I never wanted to be a villager anyway," I said with a smile.

"You scared me for a second!" Blurp said with a sigh.

"Besides, this quest wouldn't be as fun without you," I added.

I extended my hand to Blurp. He grinned and slapped it right away. We managed to become friends, so why not stay friends? People in my village are scared and narrow-minded, but I'm not! Blurp is my friend, monster or not! (Well, if he'd been an enderman, that might have been another story . . .) And we had more important things to do than fight about this little thing.

"There's no time to lose—**Mobslayer needs us!**"

"Let's go!" Blurp replied.

"I thought you looked a little weird!" I couldn't resist adding.

"**Ha ha!** No weirder than you!" Blurp said.

There was just one thing that I didn't understand. "Why would you want to be a villager?" I asked. "All they want is to trade and earn emeralds . . . But hey, I can teach you how if you want. **It's only THIRTY emeralds per lesson, HA HA!**"

87

"Then I might stay a monster after all!"

We were joking as we made our way down the cliff face, but we were both still worried. Would we find Mobslayer alive? What about the enderman? Did the fall end him, or would he be waiting for us below?

Our adventure is only just **beginning**.

THEN I MIGHT STAY A MONSTER AFTER ALL!

TO BE CONTINUED

ABOUT CUBE KID

Cube Kid is the pen name of Erik Gunnar Taylor, a writer who has lived in Alaska his whole life. A big fan of video games—especially Minecraft—he discovered early that he also had a passion for writing fan fiction.

Cube Kid's unofficial Minecraft fan fiction series, *Diary of a Wimpy Villager*, came out as e-books in 2015 and immediately met with great success in the Minecraft community. They were published in France by 404 éditions in paperback with illustrations by Saboten and now return in this same format to Cube Kid's native country under the title *Diary of an 8-Bit Warrior*.

When not writing, Cube Kid likes to travel, putter with his car, devour fan fiction, and play his favorite video game.

ABOUT THE AUTHORS

Pirate Sourcil is a comic book author known for his blog and his comic series *Le Joueur du grenier*, published by Hugo BD. He is also a fan of geek literature and passionate about the world of gaming.

After studying carpentry, **Jez** turned to drawing and graphic design and decided to make a career out of it.

Odone is a French illustrator and specializes in adding color to many comic books.

DIARY OF AN 8-BIT WARRIOR

DISCOVER THE ORIGINAL SERIES

OR ENJOY THE GRAPHIC NOVEL SERIES